WAIT YOUR TURN, GRUMPY BUNNY!

For Granny Valerie and everybunny else whose patience makes
the world a nicer place.
—J.K.F.

For Katherine and Jim...and "MainStreet BookEnds"!
—Lots of Love, Lucinda

Text copyright © 2007 by Justine Korman Fontes
Illustrations copyright © 2007 by Lucinda McQueen

All rights reserved. Published by Scholastic Inc.
SCHOLASTIC and associated logos are trademarks and/or registered trademarks of Scholastic Inc.
GRUMPY BUNNY is a trademark of Justine Korman Fontes, Lucinda McQueen, and Scholastic Inc.

ISBN-13: 978-0-439-68781-2
ISBN-10: 0-439-68781-0

12 11 10 9 8 7 6 5 4 3 2 1   7 8 9 10 11 12/0

Printed in the U.S.A.
First printing, February 2007

WAIT YOUR TURN, GRUMPY BUNNY!

by Justine Korman Fontes
Illustrated by Lucinda McQueen

SCHOLASTIC INC.

New York   Toronto   London   Auckland   Sydney
Mexico City   New Delhi   Hong Kong   Buenos Aires

Chapter 1
Hurry Up and Wait

Hopper O'Hare hurried to the bus stop.
"Worms!" he said. "School days are just
one long line."
He waited on line to get on the bus.
Then he waited on line to get off the bus.

Hopper had to wait to get a drink of water.

He had to wait to use a scooter in
gym class.

Hopper even had to wait during
arts and crafts time.
"Lilac is using the purple crayon
now," Mrs. Violet told Hopper.
"You'll have to wait."
Hopper's ears turned red.
He was sick of waiting!

Hopper had a question during story time.
He raised his paw and waited.
Hopper waited a long time.
He forgot his question!
Everyone laughed.

Chapter 2
King Hopper

Finally, it was time for recess!
Hopper couldn't wait to have some fun.
But there was a line for the swings.
"Wiggly worms!" Hopper said. "I wish
I lived somewhere without any lines."

If I were king of my own country . . .
Hopper began to daydream.
Kings never wait on line,
he thought. *Wouldn't that be great?*

Hopper thought about being first
at the water fountain,

first at the library,

and first at lunch.

It was always Hopper's turn in Hopperland!

There were no lines at the skating rink.

Chapter 3
King of the Swings

But soon, there was nobody to play with!
All of King Hopper's friends went away.
No one wanted to play with him.
Swings are no fun alone, Hopper thought.
*Even a king needs someone to give him
a push.*

The seesaw was even worse than the swings. Hopper sighed. "Toys are no fun without friends."

Hopper decided he didn't want to
be king any more.
"I'd rather wait my turn than play
alone," he said.

Chapter 4
Next!

Just then, Hopper heard Coach Parsley
shout, "Next!"
Hopper's best friend, Corny Cabbage, cried,
"Take your turn!"
"Carrots and jellybeans!" Hopper said.
"It's finally my turn!"

Hopper jumped onto the swing.
Corny started pushing.
"Higher!" Hopper squeaked. "Whee!"
Hopper swung so high he got dizzy.
And he didn't mind when his turn was over.

Hopper went to Corny's house after school.
Corny had so many brothers and sisters.
There was a line for everything!
But Hopper didn't mind.
He was glad to wait his turn.

Everyone cheered when Hopper
made a basket.
Hopper knew that having friends
was even better than being king.